CONTENTS

PROLOGUE

The nearby village was filled with bright lights and laughter, but down in the darkness, where the land met the ocean, something was stirring. A tall figure glided across the damp sand to the edge of the raging sea, the wind whipping at his scaly cloak. The stranger stopped and faced the dark water in front of him. Flinging back his head, he opened his arms out wide towards the unsettled water, his razor-sharp nails glinting in the moonlight.

"I am the Dragon King!" he bellowed. "I have returned more powerful than ever before. And no one shall defeat me!"

He was back. And this time he was going to control the creature that haunted dreams, a legend that every child knew about from the cautionary tales whispered by anxious parents.

The waves crashed into the rocks as the Dragon King held out his clawed hands towards the ocean. He opened his mouth and laughed, his pointed teeth bared.

"I summon you from the deep – dearest

creature of terror, stuff of nightmares! All of the Jade Kingdom will kneel before me when they see that you are under my command!"

Suddenly, something came rushing fast towards him beneath the water. A tsunami-like wave was forming, the water rising high as he lifted his hands into the sky. The Dragon King cackled with glee as the creature zoomed to him.

"Come, my magnificent and terrifying monster! You may have defeated me twice, Tiger Warrior, but there shall not be a third time! Soon you and the whole of the Jade Kingdom will cry in despair as I take over! Come, Nian! Rise from the deep! Together we shall rule!" he called out.

Three large wooden fishing boats bobbed uneasily on the water's surface. Then suddenly, one by one, they were pulled under. Splintered planks rose to the surface and were swept away on the ocean until they washed up in the waves at the Dragon's King's feet.

The dark clouds loomed overhead as the Dragon King's eyes widened. A gigantic, lion-like head was emerging from the waves! It had two huge horns, red eyes, a matted green mane and huge fangs dripping with saliva. The creature towered over him, so fierce and ferocious that even the Dragon King took a step back. "Welcome, Nian." The Dragon King bowed, then produced a glowing jewel from his pocket. "I have a job for you."

With the beast by his side, the Dragon King turned towards the village. His plan was coming together well.

CHAPTER ONE

"Jack, can you grab those bags of oranges from the boot of the car?" his mum asked.

It was Lunar New Year, and they had just arrived at the Chinese Community Centre for a party. There would be lots of families sharing food, a storyteller and even a Lion Dance later on. Jack was really excited – Lunar New Year's Eve was one of his favourite times of the year. He loved the bit where they pretended to eat the lettuce dangling from the doorway. And then to finish the celebrations, firecrackers would be let off and Jack and all the other kids would be given money in red envelopes called 'hongbao'. It was one tradition that Jack was especially happy about. *Who wouldn't want an envelope full of money?* Jack thought. He was hoping to save up enough for a new computer game.

"Jack!" Mum said impatiently.

Jack rushed to help. In the realm of the Jade Kingdom, he was the Tiger Warrior, a powerful hero tasked with protecting a magical land – but back in his world he

was just a normal boy expected to help his mum by carrying stuff.

"The house is clean, I've bought the decorations and the firecrackers ..." Mum was muttering to herself. Even though Mum wasn't Chinese, she made sure Jack learned about the traditions his father, Ju-Long, had celebrated. Now that his dad was no longer alive, it was up to Mum and his grandad, Yeye, to tell Jack about his Chinese heritage.

Jack had always thought that Yeye was just trying to teach him when he told him all the old myths and legends, but really Yeye had a magical secret: he was preparing Jack to become the next Tiger Warrior, just like his father and Yeye before him.

The Tiger Warrior was the guardian of a magical world called the Jade Kingdom. Yeye had given him a Jade Coin with the power of the animals of the zodiac. It was Jack's job to use their magical abilities to protect the Jade Kingdom.

Jack put the bags of oranges on the table and was about to go back to the car to unload some more things when Yeye appeared from the side door. He looked strange, like he was itching to tell Jack something. Yeye began to cross the room in Jack's direction, but Mum got there first. She threw a pile of folded square material into Jack's hands.

"Thanks, kiddo. Now can you give the red tablecloths to Mrs Wu? She's over there putting up the good luck banners above the door." She smiled and walked off to help the storyteller get set up in the corner. It was Mr Yip from the bank – he'd come dressed as the Kitchen God, wearing a fake beard and a long red robe over some trousers. Jack was on his way over to Mrs Wu when Yeye caught up with him.

"Jack, I need to talk to you ..." Yeye had a strange look in his eyes.

"Hang on a second, Yeye," said Jack as he walked over to Mrs Wu and gave her the tablecloths. Yeye was still behind him. But before Yeye could say anything, Mum reappeared and ushered Jack over to where the smaller children were sitting on a mat, waiting for Mr Yip to start telling a story.

Jack really wanted to go and eat some of Mrs Yip's jiaozi, the delicious white dumplings filled with meat and vegetables. They were Jack's favourite food and they symbolised wealth. They were particularly good to eat during the new year celebrations. Last year, he'd been too late and they'd all been eaten before he could gobble down even one. Another family had brought a whole fish with spring onions and ginger, and another had set down a large bowl filled with long yellow noodles to symbolise long life. Jack was eager to dig in, but his mum had other ideas and kept giving him jobs to do. Yeye was hovering around like a fly. Jack thought it was strange that his grandpa was following him about and not talking with the other members of the community centre like he usually did.

"I need to speak to you," said Yeye.

"The story's about to begin!" Jack's mum hushed him.

In the storytelling corner, Mr Yip started to speak. Jack had listened to the stories every year, but there was one that still sent a shiver down his spine when he heard it: "On Lunar New Year's Eve, the lion-headed beast, Nian comes," Mr Yip intoned. "The villagers decorate their houses with red banners called chunlian. Everyone gets their pots and pans ready to make noise to scare it away. Because if you didn't ... or if you didn't believe it

was coming ... it might come looking for you!"

Mr Yip gave a roar that made the children jump. It made Jack jump too, although he hoped no one had noticed.

"Then the monster would creep up to the village at night, its horns pointy and deadly. Nian would seek out quiet houses without red decorations ... its belly gurgling with hunger ... its fangs dripping with saliva! It would devour children, the juicer the better. The Nian monster had the sharpest teeth and the most jagged claws you have ever seen. If you were in its path it would SNAP! And then you would be gulped down in ONE BIG BITE!"

The group of children jumped up as Mr Yip ran around the crowd snapping his hands together. Some covered their eyes. A few others ran around the room screaming. One ran over to her mum crying.

Jack felt a shiver go up his spine.

Even though Nian was just a story, it had always made him feel uneasy. Either Mr Yip was a really good storyteller or Jack was not as tough as he thought he was. He'd fought real magical beasts before and destroyed ice dragons. Surely a little made-up story shouldn't make him feel so scared! But Jack just couldn't shake the feeling that something was wrong.

Suddenly, a bony hand gripped Jack's shoulder and made him shriek out loud. "Argh!"

A familiar laugh came from behind him. It was only Yeye. Jack breathed out a sigh of relief.

"It's you, Yeye. I thought it was ..."

Jack said. "... er ... nobody." He didn't want Yeye to know he was afraid of a story. Yeye would tease him for ever!

"It's Nian, isn't it? Are you scared of Nian?" Yeye asked, eyes wide. To Jack's surprise, Yeye was nodding. "You should be scared of him. That's what I wanted to talk to you about – it's urgent!"

Jack gulped. "Nian can't be real. No way! It's just an old fairy tale that you used to tell me as part of the Lunar New Year. Isn't it?" Jack asked.

Yeye shook his head. "I thought you

were a fast learner, my boy. All of those stories I told you, they were based on some kind of truth. This is no different."

Jack knew his job as the new Tiger Warrior was to protect the Jade Kingdom against evil demons and horrible creatures trying to take over the Jade Emperor's realm. He and Princess Li, who could transform into the not-so-mythical phoenix Fenghuang, had fought together a few times now. But none of those strange creatures from the stories scared him as much as the legend of Nian.

"So, you're telling me ... that Nian ... IS real?" Jack asked. He didn't really want to hear the answer. He already knew what Yeye was going to say.

Yeye nodded. "It's as real as me. It'll be coming to the Jade Kingdom tonight, as it does every year – and it's up to you to stop it!"

CHAPTER TWO

Mr Yip was chuckling to himself as the parents gathered up the crying children. Jack followed Yeye towards the doorway, but just then his mum appeared. "Where are you two going?" she said. "We're about to eat."

Yeye looked at her with an innocent face, "Oh, we're just going to the car to bring in some more ... um ..."

"... decorations," added Jack quickly.

"All right then, but don't be too long or the food will get cold – you don't want to miss out on the jiaozi like last year," said Jack's mum, smiling. Jack certainly didn't. Luckily time passed differently in the Jade Kingdom, so hopefully he'd be back long before the food was gone. Jack could feel butterflies in his belly as he and Yeye headed outside. He didn't know if he was hungry with the thought of missing out on the dumplings, or if he was nervous about facing a creature as terrifying as Nian.

"Right, let's see what's going on in the Jade Kingdom," said Yeye. Jack nodded and got out the Jade Coin from his pocket.

The jade was cool in his hand and the images of the twelve carved animals glistened. Jack made sure no one else was outside apart from him and Yeye. Stuff like this was going to be hard to explain if they got caught.

He tossed the coin high into the air. "JADE KINGDOM!" Jack shouted. The coin turned and turned in the air, opening the familiar circular portal to the fantastic Jade Kingdom. Light flashed around the edges as it grew and grew until it was big enough for him to step through.

Yeye and Jack peered into the large spiral as the window to the other world opened up. The streets were full of

people watching dance troupes and acrobats performing – the Lunar New Year's Eve celebrations were much bigger there – and much more exciting!

"Good luck and be careful!" Yeye said, patting Jack's back.

"I'll be back for the jiaozi!" Jack laughed nervously. *If Nian doesn't eat me in one big bite ...*

Jack stepped through and the portal closed behind him. The quiet of the car park was replaced with noisy chatter and the banging of pots.

Jack could see the Lunar New Year red decorations and the streets buzzing with the marketplace full of crowds. Every door was covered with red and gold good luck banners. Red lanterns lined the streets, hung from post to post. Drummers banged big round-bottomed drums and people let off firecrackers in alleyways.

There were street market stalls set up with delicious treats to buy – custard cakes, fried dough, glazed fruit on sticks. Jack glanced at groups of children playing all around the marketplace. Some were kicking a smooth stone ball; a brother and sister were playing hide-and-seek among the stalls. Jack saw three children sitting watching a shadow play.

As he watched, dancers under a fancy silk costume made up to look like Nian bounded around the streets to the sounds of the drums. The colourful creature looked harmless enough. It shuffled up high and caught a lettuce then shredded it, throwing the leaves everywhere.

Children laughed and ran around trying not to be caught by the dancing lion creature.

But amongst all the noise and fun, Jack could feel the tension. Parents were keeping an eye on their young ones. Smiles were betrayed by eyes searching for trouble.

Jack held out the coin. "ZODIAC!" he shouted. In an instant his twelve companions, the zodiac animals, were by his side, glowing with magical power. Rabbit immediately hid behind Jack's leg, cowering away from the crowd and loud noises of firecrackers and drums. Jack picked him up and stroked his furry head.

"It's OK, they won't hurt you." He put Rabbit back on the floor.

Dog was wagging his tail and looking around at the celebrations.

"It's a brilliant party!" he said. "Hey, Pig, don't go eating ALL of the food now will you, save some for everyone else! We've got a long night ahead. We'll need to keep our wits about us."

"That's why it's important to fill up on treats now," Pig said. "Ohhh, look! Spring onion pancakes!" Pig snorted his way over to a stall.

Jack looked around for Goat, the telepathic one of the bunch of animals. "Hey, Goat ..."

"Yes, I know, I know ... you want me to send a message to Princess Li. Put your hand on my back." Jack did as he was told. He still wasn't that good at using Goat's power but he tried to concentrate hard. *Li! Meet me in the marketplace,* he thought, hoping that the message got through.

Snake slithered her way around Jack's leg up to his shoulder and whispered in his ear. "It's so niccce to be back," she said. "Every Lunar New Year we come here to ward off Nian. Your father alwaysss did a fine job of protecting the citizens from Nian." Snake looked sad for a moment. Jack felt the same. When he had found out he was the Tiger Warrior, he also found out that his father, Ju-Long, had been killed by the Dragon King – the enemy of the Jade Emperor and now also Jack's enemy. Yeye had taken over as Tiger Warrior again after his son had died, but now Jack had taken his place. Yeye was getting too old for this kind of adventure.

Jack took a deep breath. Now it was his turn to work with the zodiac animals to keep all the people of the Jade Kingdom safe.

"Speaking of Ju-Long – Jack, come here!" Pig said, excitedly. "These little buns with red bean paste were your father's favourite treat. Here, try some."

Jack took the bun from the stall and took a bite – it was delicious and not too sweet.

"Yum!" said Jack, wiping his mouth. It was nice to try something that his father had liked. But his enjoyment was soon interrupted. People began looking up into the sky and pointing. Jack and the animals gazed up to see what was going on.

Up in the sky, a shadowy figure flew overhead. Jack's hands automatically went to the Jade Coin in his pocket, ready for battle. But as the wings of the creature spread out to land, Jack finally recognised who it was. It was the Fenghuang –

Princess Li in the form of the phoenix! As her feet touched the ground, the bird span and suddenly there in its place was Princess Li, dressed in a red and gold qi-pao dress. She ran over and high-fived Jack.

"I'm so glad you're here! You're going

to love the Lunar New Year celebrations in the Jade Kingdom."

"I'm glad to be here," he said, feeling a little uneasy. He thought about what Yeye and the zodiac animals had told him. He was supposed to ward off Nian. How could he enjoy the festivities when he had such an important job to do?

"Where's the Jade Emperor?" Jack asked.

"Father is in the Heavenly Realm at the moment. That's why I'm in charge! I'm hoping we won't have any trouble and we can just enjoy ourselves. We know how to scare Nian off: red and noise. I've put up red signs and decorations all over the village, and everyone knows to make as much noise as possible."

"We're here to help too!" added Dog. The rest of the animals nodded in agreement. Jack looked at the zodiac animals. They were poised and ready for action. Well, apart from Pig, who was wandering from stall to stall eating lots of delicious food.

"Relax, Jack! I've sorted it." Li laughed. "Just have some fun! Everything will be fine. We've been scaring Nian away for centuries."

Then, as if there had been a power cut, everything went pitch black. The lights from the many lanterns had all gone off. The villagers began screaming and moving away from the marketplace, shoving and jostling each other. The sound of ripping paper could be heard all around.

"The decorations that keep Nian away are being shredded!" someone yelled out.

"What can we do?" said Jack. He wasn't sure what they could do in darkness. Rabbit trembled by his leg.

"Uh oh," said Goat, "I've got a very bad feeling."

Suddenly, flashes of light pierced the sky. A familiar voice boomed out around the marketplace.

"The party is over!" the Dragon King declared. "Nian is back. And tonight, he will feast!"

CHAPTER THREE

The vibrant marketplace was plunged into shadowy darkness.

"Ouch!" Pig snorted. "Something hit my trotter."

"We need to get some light around here." Jack peered through the gloom. Everyone was trying to escape to their homes. But as well as being strangely dark, it was also oddly quiet. A weird hush was sweeping over the marketplace. As Jack watched, an old woman raced by, clutching a candle. Her mouth was open, but hardly a sound was coming out of it. What should have been cries of fear were now only whispers.

Jack tried to shout to Li. But something was wrong with his throat. His shout came out of his mouth as a whisper. It was as if the volume dial had been turned down to low.

"TIGER!" Jack commanded. Even though his voice was low and hard to hear, Tiger was by his side in an instant. "We need firebolts to light up the sky – at least then we can see what we're dealing with," said Jack, straining his voice to be heard. He placed his hand on Tiger's back. Tiger shot large balls of fire into the night sky, illuminating the darkened village. The flare-like flames helped Jack to see what was going on. Many of the villagers were cowering in corners, many had fled in the darkness.

Jack and the animals ran over to Li,

who was helping an old man to his feet.

Jack's voice was barely a whisper. "Why can't I speak properly?" Jack put a hand on his throat, his face worried.

Li whispered back. "Dark magic – it's the Dragon King, I think he's cast a spell on us to be quiet. Nian is scared by loud noises. The Dragon King has forced us all to be quiet like mice."

"But we can still make noise with the drums over there to keep the beast away," said Monkey.

Li nodded and ran over to the place where the drummers had left their instruments. But as she lifted her arms to bang the drum, the Dragon King appeared on top of a nearby roof. Jack felt angry seeing the man who had killed his father so near to him.

The Dragon King held up a bright orange jewel and cackled quietly. No matter how hard Li struck the drum with the stick, no sound could be heard. The sound was sucked up by the jewel. Furious, Li kept beating the drum until it broke, and then threw it up at the Dragon King, who just laughed as the drum smashed near him soundlessly.

Jack watched as the Dragon King bent down and touched the jewel to a red lantern dangling from the roof where he was standing. The red colour began

to turn black. Li looked down at her dress as it turned black too. The Dragon King laughed and transformed into his dragon form.

Jack and Li watched as the shadowy figure flew away from the rooftop, taking the orange jewel with him.

Li and Jack looked around at the village. The orange jewel had not only sucked up all of the colour red from the village, it had also taken away their ability to shout and scream. *This is bad, very bad,* thought Jack. They were the two things that kept Nian away. Jack felt the rage bubble up inside of him as he thought about the Dragon King and his evil ways.

"I'm going after him!" Jack was about to flip the coin and summon Horse when a man ran towards them, waving desperately at Jack and Li.

"What's the matter?" Jack whispered.

The terror in the man's eyes told him what it was even before the words left the man's mouth.

"Nian's coming! It's too late!"

Jack and Li turned, ready to fight, as the monster approached. Its sharp fangs shone in the firelight, its eyes wild with hunger. It was bigger and more terrifying than Jack had imagined. It had two long spikes on its head poking out of its bright green fur, and four large fangs framed its terrifying mouth. A long tail swished from side to side. Windows and doors were quickly locked tight. The streets were cleared of people as they cowered indoors.

Jack's hands began to shake with nerves. But as they did, he felt Tiger's fur and it gave him an idea.

"Li, Tiger's firebolts are red and the

Dragon King's magic hasn't stopped them from zooming into the sky. Let's gather everyone in one place and we can protect them with the red light of the fire. That should keep the people safe until we can deal with Nian."

"Great idea! Let's get them to the town hall, quickly," said Li. Jack, Li and the animals began herding people to the central hall. Jack and Tiger created a fire perimeter to keep the villagers safe inside. Li was about to lock the outer door when a woman came running through it, frantic tears streaming down her face.

"You have to help me!" she gasped.

“I can’t find my three children. They were watching the shadow play. Nian will eat them – please, you have to find them!” she whispered desperately.

A huge roar outside made everyone in the hall quiver with fear. For a second, Jack froze as chills went down his spine. Li nudged his arm and snapped him out of it. “We have to help the children!”

“You’re right. Let’s go get them!” Jack said as bravely as he could. He took a deep breath and looked at the zodiac animals and Li, who were all standing next to him, looking at him expectantly. Could they tell how scared he was inside?

CHAPTER FOUR

Jack unbolted the door and peered out into the flickering light of the fire beacons they'd set up around the hall. They were working to keep Nian away – but there were kids out there, away from the protection of the glowing red fire.

"Come on!" Li burst out into the street, looking out for the lion-headed beast.

"I've got a plan," said Jack. "Snake, Li

and I need to get closer to Nian without him seeing us, can you help?"

"Sure ... I can ... sssss." Snake did as Jack asked. She wound herself around Jack's arm like a tight bracelet, giving him her power of invisibility. Jack grabbed Li's hand, making her invisible too. The three of them followed the loud roars.

"Over there," Li whispered to Jack. Jack looked over and there it was – Nian. It turned a corner and appeared like a bad nightmare, just as fearsome as it had been before.

Li led them closer to the beast. Jack tripped forward. As they crept closer the beast turned to face them, sniffing the air in their direction. It couldn't see them ... but could it smell them?

Jack could feel the stinking hot breath of the beast on his cheeks. It was like smelly cooked garbage. Jack gulped. His whole body was shaking with fear, and he was feeling less like a warrior, more like one of the scared kids listening to Mr Yip's stories back home. But here the beast was real, and it was so near they could almost touch noses. Jack could feel himself begin to have cold chills. He hadn't fully mastered Snake's power yet. As he thought about the times the invisibility had failed before, his arm started to shake.

"Jaaccck," Snake hissed as her power faded. Jack and Li were exposed. Nian was looking right at them!

Li spun around with no time to spare as Nian roared a mighty roar. Its mouth was cavernous. Jack froze to the spot. Luckily Li swept into action. As Nian lunged she flipped into the air and transformed into

her Fenghuang form, pushing Jack out of harm's way with one feathery wing. She flew up high and gathered momentum, then dived down into the beast. Nian crashed into a market stall but was up on its feet again in seconds, growling viciously. The Fenghuang shot lightning strikes from the tips of her wings into Nian's side.

Jack ran for cover behind an overturned cart, panting for breath. He didn't know why he felt so scared – he hadn't felt like this when he faced the fox demons, or even the Dragon King. But Nian was the creature of his childhood nightmares, and something about him flooded Jack with fear ... He tried to get the coin from his pocket, but his fingers felt like jelly and he dropped it. It rolled away on its side into the darkness. Jack slapped his forehead. How could he drop the coin at a time like this!

Jack panicked and looked to see how Li was doing. She was totally brave, not like him. He didn't know what had come over him. He thought he'd learned courage and bravery from fearless Tiger, but somehow all that training had disappeared and he was acting more nervous than Rabbit.

"Come on, Jack, get it together. The Jade Kingdom needs you," Jack told himself.

The Fenghuang sent another lightning bolt towards Nian. It dodged, but the sparks ignited a hay bale on a market stall. The fire burned bright red, making Nian howl with pain, his lion-like face lit up by the blazing flames. As the red fire raged, Nian turned and ran away.

Jack breathed a shaky sigh of relief. The beast had fled the marketplace for now, but for how long?

Jack had to find the precious Jade Coin. Without it, he would be no help whatsoever. He got on his hands and knees in the area where he had seen it roll away. He patted his hands all around the floor trying to find it.

"Thank goodness I didn't lose the coin," he muttered as he saw it glinting beside a basket of firewood.

A battered and bruised Li rushed over to him.

"What happened to you? I could have done with some backup," she whispered. Her wrist was bleeding from her fight with Nian.

"I'm sorry, Li, I ... erm ... the Jade

Coin fell." Jack felt bad for giving her excuses. He didn't want to tell her he was having trouble being brave.

"I couldn't take him on by myself. He got me good – here and here." Li lifted up her wrist and pointed to her leg, where blood was dripping from deep cuts.

"Wait, I can help you with that," Jack said. "DOG!" Jack transformed into Dog, the healing zodiac animal. As Dog, Jack gently placed his paws on Li's cuts and healing light flooded her body. They watched as her wounds disappeared in an instant.

"Thanks, that feels back to normal,"

said Li as Jack changed back into his own human form.

"At least there's something I can do," Jack muttered to himself. His hands were still shaking. He sat on the side of a well. Li pulled up a bucket full of water and gulped it down.

"Have a sip of water, Jack. It might

help calm your nerves," said Horse. Jack realised he couldn't hide how he was feeling from Li or the zodiac animals. They all crowded round and spoke as loudly as they could – which was still just a whisper thanks to the Dragon King's spell.

"I'm sorry I didn't fight. It's just, the story of Nian has always terrified me and seeing him in real life made me feel …" Jack paused, worried they wouldn't think he was worthy of being the Tiger Warrior any more. "I felt so scared. I know that's not what warriors are meant to be like."

"It's OK," said Li kindly, "there are all kinds of warriors."

Rabbit hopped over to Jack and sat on his lap. "You can't help being scared," he said.

Dragon moved to Jack's side too. "Rabbit is right, everyone gets scared sometimes. Even me!" The other zodiac animals nodded their heads in agreement.

Pig was eating a stray candied apple that had fallen from a stall. "I remember that battle when your dad was fighting the Dragon King. I was very afraid. I didn't eat for a whole hour afterwards."

Rooster began tapping the side of the well with his beak.

"Rooster is telling us about the time

we were trapped in a dark deep cave," said Ox. "Your grandpa had been trapped by a flying demon. I managed to bulldoze our way out, but Rooster has never forgotten it."

Jack still felt bad. "At least I'm not as nervous as Rabbit," he joked. The zodiac animals looked at him and Jack felt ashamed. Rabbit hopped off his lap and went over to hide by Dragon.

"Rabbit might be the most timid of our group, but he has very strong powers. It's not always the most obvious creatures that are the most powerful," Dragon said, nodding wisely.

"Sorry, Rabbit, I didn't mean—" Jack

started. He was getting everything wrong today.

"Come on, we have to find the missing kids," Li said. She stood up, looking much better. Her wounds had been completely healed. Jack could see she was raring to go, unlike him. "If only we could shout so they could hear us!" she added.

"We need to get the orange jewel from the Dragon King. Without it we have no chance against Nian," Jack said. "Zodiac animals, go spread out and find the missing three children. The mother said they were in the marketplace at the shadow puppet stand." With that command, Dragon soared high in the sky, darting in between the streets. Monkey set off by climbing to the top of the tallest nearby building. Jack watched him swinging from one string of lanterns to another, checking inside windows as he moved. Dog padded around and sniffed open doorways. Rat scurried into holes and crevices looking for signs of the missing children. Jack wandered around, calling as loud as he could, straining to make his voice heard. "Children, where are you?"

Li rushed off in the opposite direction.

Jack rounded the corner and saw lots of overturned stalls. He lifted one up to see if the children were hiding underneath, but instead found Rabbit in there.

"Oh, Rabbit!" he stuttered. "I'm sorry about what I said. I know you have amazing jumping power." As he said it, Jack realised he'd never seen Rabbit's jumping power. Yeye had always said that Rabbit would show him when he was ready. "In fact, that could come in useful now. If I could jump, I could see much more of the marketplace and try to spot the kids." Rabbit shrank back under the stall even further.

"Please, Rabbit, I'm really sorry I was mean – I was feeling bad and I took it out on you. But I need your help," Jack said.

"Real bravery isn't not being scared," Rabbit whispered. "It's being scared but doing it anyway, because it's the right thing to do." Rabbit crept out and stood in front of Jack. "You can pick me up," he said. Jack carefully put his hands around Rabbit's warm furry back and tucked him under his arm. As Rabbit quivered under his arm, Jack felt his hand charge with power. Then his whole body. His legs felt super-charged.

"Now you can jump!" said Rabbit with glee, sounding happy to have shared his talent with Jack. Jack grinned and began hopping with both legs at a time. He jumped long and wide all over the marketplace, searching for the kids as he went. He bounded like a kangaroo. His legs felt amazing. He was having so much fun he almost forgot to be scared of Nian – until something huge and scaly turned the corner in front of him.

Luckily it was only Dragon! Dragon

laughed as Jack jumped as high as he could. When he landed, the earth underneath trembled and the rickety buildings rattled.

"That was amazing!" Jack gasped.

"That's nothing compared to Rabbit's full power. If you can align with Rabbit's spirit and transform, you will feel the full force of the earthquake hop," Dragon told him.

"Wow," whispered Jack as he put Rabbit down. "Your power is amazing. My legs were so strong." He bent down and stroked the small creature's long ears. "You have brilliant power, and I won't forget what you said."

Rabbit's ears lifted up, pleased to hear Jack's words.

Jack suddenly heard a familiar voice sounding in his head. It was Goat using her telepathy.

"I've found the children," Goat's voice

echoed in his head. "They're by the old rice store in the east of the village – but hurry! Nian is coming!"

CHAPTER FIVE

Jack quickly picked up Rabbit and hopped towards the east of the village using great leaping bounds. Goat was rummaging around in the wreckage of a rice store which had been damaged by Nian's rampage.

"Baaaa! The wall is about to fall," Goat told Jack as he bounced over.

A building had been destroyed, and the

one remaining wall was teetering above the remains of a stall.

"Help us!" Jack could hear tiny voices coming from the pile as the children cried and coughed. "Please, someone!"

"Don't worry, I'm coming," Jack said as loudly as he could.

Jack saw Li flying high overhead in her Fenghuang form, still looking for the missing children.

"Over here!" Jack tried to shout. He waved his hands in the air, hoping to catch her attention. But she flew overhead without noticing him.

"Goat, come here," Jack said, putting Rabbit down. He put his hands on Goat's back and felt her power flood through him. Then he began trying to connect with Li's mind telepathically.

"Li, I need your help. The children are trapped in the rice store under a mound of fallen rocks and wooden planks. I'm going to use Ox's strength to move it, but you have to get them out while I hold it all up. Otherwise it could all collapse on them. Please come fast!" Jack said. He peered up into the sky, hoping she'd heard. As they watched, the Fenghuang, the majestic phoenix, turned and started flying down towards where Jack and the animals were waiting. Jack didn't waste any time.

"OX!" he summoned, flicking the Jade Coin high into the air. Ox appeared out of the coin and Jack climbed up onto her broad back. As Li landed, Ox's strength flooded into Jack and he held the wooden timbers and huge pieces of rubble out of the way so that the three trapped children could be seen. As he did, the

Fenghuang swooped down and, with her talons, carefully lifted each kid to safety – and just in time. As Jack let go of Ox, the wall smashed down, covering them all in a layer of dust.

"Thank you for saving us!" said the oldest boy.

"We were hiding from Nian," said the girl.

"But he tried to get us and the building fell. We were really scared," said the little one.

Suddenly, a shadow loomed large onto a nearby wall – and this time it wasn't Dragon! Nian was coming back.

"Snake!" Jack flipped the coin and all

the other animals disappeared. Snake wrapped around his arm. Then he and Li got the children to all hold hands. He held the eldest boy's hands and they all disappeared. But keeping so many people invisible was not easy using Snake's power. Nian walked past, sniffing the air, and everyone held their breath.

As Nian turned the corner, Snake gave a deep sigh and let go of Jack's arm. Everyone who had been hiding from the beast reappeared. They all sighed, relieved they hadn't been found.

But just as Jack felt relieved, he heard a voice that sent a chill down his spine.

"Ah, Nian!" it called. "My faithful

friend." It was the Dragon King!

"Stay here!" Jack whispered to the children. Li was already creeping ahead. He followed her and they peered around a corner to see Nian and the Dragon King in the middle of the marketplace, next to a statue of the Jade Emperor.

"The villagers cannot keep you at bay now there are no more red decorations to ward you off, and I have taken all of the loud noises from their mouths. There is only a small amount of red left!" The Dragon King gave a low laugh as he pointed at the orange jewel which was floating in mid-air above them.

The Dragon King laughed again, baring

his jagged teeth.

"We are nearly there! The jewel has almost finished taking in all of the things that could harm you. When we're done here, you will be unleashed on the whole of the Jade Kingdom!" he cackled.

Jack looked at Li. Her eyes were wide.

"We have to get that jewel," Li whispered. "We need to smash it and then the colour and sound will return. It's the only way we can drive Nian away."

Jack nodded. "But how can we get close enough to break it?" he asked. "If only I could use Snake properly, but I can only stay invisible for a short while."

"I've got it!" said Li. She ran over to the side of the marketplace where the huge Nian costume had been discarded by the performers in the ruckus. "We can pretend to be Nian and get close enough to snatch the jewel."

"Sounds like the only plan we have right now," said Jack. "I'm in."

"Us too," said the three children.

"ZODIAC!" Jack whispered. The animals all appeared and Jack quickly explained his plan.

"He'll never believe that bunch of rags is Nian!" Dog exclaimed.

"I can help with that," Goat offered.

The costume was big and long. Jack, Li, the children and the zodiac animals scrambled inside.

"Now we just need to get the real Nian away," Li said. "Monkey, can you cause a diversion?" Monkey nodded and scampered away. Seconds later a huge crash came from the other side of the marketplace. The Dragon King nodded at Nian and it went to investigate. As soon as it was out of sight, the fake Nian quickly got ready.

"Excuse me! How rude! You stood on

my hoof!" muttered Goat.

"I wanted to be at the front of the costume," hissed Rat.

"Shushhh!!! Try to walk in time with each other!" said Jack. He wasn't sure this was going to work.

"We look like a Nian with a belly full of animals," giggled Dog. The other animals laughed.

But Jack didn't. He could feel his fear coming back. His stomach was knotted and his hands were shaking. The fake Nian rounded the corner and stood in front of the Dragon King.

Jack held on to Goat and thought, *I am Nian*, as hard as he could, projecting the

thought into the Dragon King's mind.

The Dragon King looked at the costume and a confused look came over his face.

I am Nian, I am Nian, Jack thought even harder.

The Dragon King shook his head and his eyebrows furrowed.

Goat bleated in Jack's ear. "Quick, he's

getting suspicious. We need to grab the jewel now!"

Everything happened in a blur.

Li reached her hand out from under the costume. At the same time Jack threw off the costume and reached for the coin. "Tiger Transform!" he whispered. Jack leapt into the air but landed neatly on his tiger paws in front of the Dragon King, his arch enemy.

Li dived for the orange jewel but it was too late. The Dragon King had taken it into his claws. He grabbed her in his other arm and smashed her down to the ground. Li changed into her human form, looking tiny next to the Dragon King's great foot. She groaned weakly, but didn't get up. The Dragon King gave a cruel laugh and turned to leer at the costume where the three children were still trapped.

"Haha! Succulent little children – perfect for Nian's feeding time!"

The three children screamed.

"Let them go!" Jack roared. He could feel the fur on his back prickle. His blood went cold.

"Ahhh, just in time for dinner! A new year's feast indeed!" the Dragon King said as Jack felt a huge presence behind him.

CHAPTER SIX

Drool dripped from Nian's fangs as it headed towards the three children.

Jack gulped but knew it was up to him. He stood in front of them, his tiger tail twitching with fear. His belly gurgled, his whole body began to shake. He imagined himself running away and hiding in a haystack. But then he saw the zodiac animals. Rabbit was tapping his long foot on the ground nervously and Jack remembered what Rabbit had said earlier.

It didn't matter that he was scared. It wasn't about getting rid of the nerves but using them to do what was right. It was no use to anyone if he ran away – Nian and the Dragon King would win. He could be scared AND fight.

Rabbit hopped onto Jack's shoulder and whispered into Jack's ear.

"You can do it, Jack! I believe in you. You are brave," Rabbit said.

"As brave as a rabbit," Jack said, looking down at Rabbit. He felt terrified, but he couldn't let Nian win. For the kids, for his friends, for the whole Jade

Kingdom – he would fight even if his hands shook the whole time. Rabbit nodded, and Jack felt the sense he'd felt before with Tiger and Dog, as he connected with the true spirit of a zodiac animal.

Jack shouted, "RABBIT!" and fully transformed into rabbit form. He felt the power surge into his body. He and Rabbit were one.

Without thinking, Jack jumped onto Nian's back, avoiding the huge spikey horns on the monster's head. Its furry mane smelled like dirty feet and sewers.

"Run!" Jack said to the kids.

The three children ran as fast as their

feet would carry them away from the fighting to hide under an upturned cart. They watched through gaps in the wood. Jack glanced over and saw the smallest child being brave and poking her head out to the side to get a better look. Her brother was dragging her back behind the cart.

Jack pounded Nian's head with his long furry feet. He pulled on Nian's green mane, which felt like course hay. Nian spun and snapped, trying to spear him with its huge horns or crunch him in its jagged teeth.

But Jack was too fast. He bounced up and down, using his strong rabbit feet to give Nian the biggest headache. The beast spun, trying to swat Jack like a fly on its back. Nian growled and bucked some more. It was getting frustrated and tired. Round and round it spun, like a mechanical bull at a rodeo, jerking this way and that, trying to catch the little rabbit hopping on its dizzy head.

Jack knew he could carry on like this for ever – the power of Rabbit's amazing hop felt infinite. Nian's head went round and round like a washing machine drum. Its eyes were moving in all sorts of funny directions. Finally Nian slid to the side and tripped over its own very long tail, its whole body flying into the air and smashing into the statue of the Jade Emperor. *BOFF!*

Jack hopped down, ready for the next stage of the battle, but Nian was lying unconscious on the floor. He'd done it! But before he could celebrate, a mocking laugh ran out across the square.

Jack turned to look at the Dragon King and felt fury bubble up inside him. This was his chance to get revenge on the Dragon King once and for all. Jack hadn't forgotten who had killed his father, and who had hurt his friend. He glanced over at where Li was still lying on the floor. He wanted to go to her and help – but first the Dragon King would pay.

Jack stood in front of his enemy. However, the Dragon King merely threw his head back and laughed again, showing his glistening teeth.

"As if a puny bunny can defeat me. Go back to your burrow!"

Jack could feel his nose twitching. How dare the Dragon King speak to him like that! Jack used his rabbit power to jump as high as he could into the air. He could feel the power building in his small furry body. *Let's see who's puny!* Jack thought as he smashed back down. *EARTHQUAKE HOP!*

As his feet landed on the ground, the earth beneath him juddered. The paving began to move, and a huge crack spread out from Jack's feet across the square.

The crack began to open wider and wider until a crevasse appeared at the evil demon's feet.

At the same time, the Fenghuang woke up and twisted out of his clutches, lifting her wings and flying high into the night sky, just as the ground below the Dragon King melted away and he plummeted down into the abyss. The ground rumbled and shook more. Jack raced forward to look over the edge and saw the Dragon King struggling to hold on to a small ledge. The demon tried to use his long nails to climb back up, but it was no use. His hands began to slide down the rock face. He was falling.

"I'll be back!" he screeched as he fell into the dark hole, his claws still scratching the side of the earth.

CHAPTER SEVEN

As Li landed, Jack hopped over the crevasse in one bound and rushed over to her. Bird and rabbit looked at each other, then they both transformed back into their human forms. Li shook her head dizzily. "You did it, Jack!"

Jack grinned."We still have to deal with Nian." He nodded over at where the lion beast was still unconscious, laid out on the floor. Around him the children were jumping about in relief and triumph in the corner of the marketplace.

"Hooray, we've won," one of them said. His voice was still low in volume. He looked at his siblings and held his throat. "But we still can't shout!"

"It's not over yet," said Li. "We need to break the jewel that has stolen the red and taken our loud voices and noises."

"I'm going to smash that jewel once and for all!" said Jack.

Li transformed into her Fenghuang form and opened her wings wide in front of the children.

"Don't worry, I'll protect the children,

you hop to it!" Li urged.

Jack quickly changed into his rabbit form and leapt back over the crevasse to where the orange jewel was still hovering in the air. With one almighty jump he smashed down on the jewel with all of his might, slamming it hard against the paving stones. A loud cracking sound could be heard like thunder as the ground shook once again.

Thousands of pieces of the precious jewel were scattered all over the place.

"Did you hear that?" shouted Li, "Noise! Sound has returned to the village!"

"We can laugh out loud again," said one of the children, grinning widely.

"We can YELL TOO!" cried the smallest child, peeking around the Fenghuang's feathers. Li ushered the children out from behind her then transformed into her human form. As she did, her outfit was restored to its blood red colour. Red flowed back into the village like a wave of colour washing over the buildings and signs. The decorations that hadn't been destroyed returned to their bright red and gold hues. The lanterns swayed on their ropes, bringing colour back to the night skies. The children began to clap their hands in glee. Suddenly, the doors of the town hall were flung open and people and noise spilled out into the square.

Jack transformed back into his human body. He looked down as his furry feet changed into his white and red trainers again. Then he threw back his head and yelled, "WAHOOO!" It felt so good to be able to shout again.

Just then, the beast began to stir. Nian had only been knocked out for a short while. The horns on its head lifted as it began to push itself up to all fours, shaking its terrifying head, trying to shake off its sleepiness.

"Come on, now we can scare it away! It will be the biggest Lunar New Year celebration EVER!" said Jack, picking up a discarded drum and drumstick. He began to beat it loudly. The children picked up

things they could use to make noise. The villagers started to trickle through the streets, shouting, clapping their hands, whistling, beating metal gongs. The noise was loud – and it was working. Nian gave a pained roar as it got up onto its feet and began backing away from the village. Jack and Li led the villagers as they drove out the beast. It turned as the noise became deafening and ran into the night, its tail between its legs. As soon as it was out of sight, the villagers all cheered. Their Lunar New Year celebration had not been the one they had wanted, but they were all still alive and grateful. Jack watched as the three kids rushed over to their parents and their mum hugged them tight.

"I was so worried about you all," she told them. "Thank you so much," she said to Li and Jack.

"You're welcome," said Li.

Families gathered and hugged each other in the marketplace once again. It was going to be a night to remember. It had been a very close call indeed, thought Jack.

"Nian will return next year," said Li, looking at Jack.

"But we'll be ready for him!" said Jack, grinning. "Even if we're scared."

The zodiac animals appeared and

nodded. Jack, Li and the animals gathered around the large crevasse that had opened up in the earth.

"Looks like you made a bit of a mess here," said Dog. "We can't take you anywhere, Jack!" he laughed.

Rooster was strutting around the edges. Jack grabbed him before he toppled over. "Whoa, Rooster, look where you're going or you'll be joining the Dragon King – way down there!"

Rabbit shyly came around to the front of the crowd.

"You did a great job, Rabbit," said Dragon. Jack wondered if Rabbit was blushing underneath his grey fur.

"Yes, Rabbit, excellent hopping today," said Monkey, who was swinging from the poles, holding on to the lanterns.

"What can we do about that big hole?" asked Ox in her slow voice.

"Don't worry, I'll get my father to sort it out when he's back from his trip to the Heavenly Realm," Li said. "He can fix it in a click of his fingers."

"Do you think the Dragon King is gone for good?" asked Jack, wondering if he'd finally avenged his father's death.

"I doubt it. He's probably slipped into one of the other realms," Li said. "I'm sure he'll be back, and when he does return we'll be ready for him!" Li said,

holding out her hand to high-five Jack. He slapped his palm against her hand.

"We'll all be ready to fight," said Dragon. The rest of the zodiac animals nodded in agreement.

"Enjoy the celebrations!" Jack said. The villagers had already started the party, with wild music filling the streets.

The kids had even picked up the Nian costume as they excitedly told their friends what had happened. Stalls were turned upright and the New Year festivities began again.

"Thanks, Jack," Li said as she looked round at it all.

"No problem. I am the Tiger Warrior after all," said Jack. "And after tonight, I'm a much braver Tiger Warrior. If I can face Nian, I can face anybody!"

The villagers waved goodbye. Jack waved to them all then flipped the Jade Coin into the air. "HOME!" he shouted. The portal back to his own world opened wide. Jack knew time stood still back home, and so he would still have time to eat some jiaozi. His tummy rumbled. He was barely though the portal when he spotted Yeye standing in the same spot outside the community centre where he had left him. Yeye rushed over.

"Are you all right?" He brushed Jack's hair out of his face. "I was worried about this mission. Nian has always had a strange effect on you. But you were the only one who could fight him." He slid his arm around Jack's shoulder. "Tell me all about it!" he urged. Jack smiled and walked with Yeye back into the hall.

"Nian was huge! Much bigger than in the stories. Three times the size of Ox, and you never mentioned the smell – he really stank! Even his mane was pongy!" said Jack. "I jumped on his head as Rabbit, and he couldn't fight me because I was so small and fast."

"Ahhh, good, good. Rabbit is underestimated because he's small. I remember the first time I used the earthquake hop – it was against a fire-breathing spider."

"A fire-breathing spider? Nah, that doesn't sound as scary as Nian," laughed Jack.

"It's not a contest, Jack. I was the Tiger Warrior back then, you are the Tiger Warrior now. That's all," Yeye said.

"Although the fire-breathing spider could take Nian out with one leg."

Jack laughed. As they walked back into the hall, the aroma of the tasty meat and vegetable dumplings made his mouth water. He felt ravenous, hungry as Nian. He could gobble up anything in his path.

Jack ran over to his mum, who passed him a bowl and a pair of chopsticks.

"Just in time for jiaozi!" she beamed.

"I'm starving!" replied Jack. He knew

he should enjoy these moments as much as possible. Even though the Dragon King was gone for now, like Nian, he would be back – but Jack would be ready!

THE END

ANIMAL CHARACTERISTICS

RAT

Rats might have a bit of a bad reputation in books and films, but they're number one when it comes to the zodiac. People born in the Year of the Rat are quick-witted, persuasive and very smart. They have excellent taste but can be known to be a little greedy!

OX

The Ox is patient and powerful. People born in this year are known for being kind to others. While they can be a little stubborn, people born in the Year of Ox make the best friends – they can always be counted on to protect the ones that they love.

TIGER

Tigers are famously strong and majestic, so it's no wonder that Tiger Warriors like Jack and his yeye are born in this year. People born in the Year of the Tiger are courageous but are known to be a bit moody, too!

RABBIT

Forget the cute bunnies, people born in the Year of the Rabbit are the cool kids! Known for being popular, sincere and for always helping others, you're likely to find rabbits at home with lots of guests around.

DRAGON

If you're born in this year, you're very lucky indeed! The charismatic dragon is revered all over China. Those born in the Year of the Dragon are energetic and fearless, but can be a bit selfish ... No wonder the Dragon King thinks he should be the leader of the Jade Kingdom!

SNAKE

Those born in the Year of the Sssnake are quiet, charming and smart. They're very good with money, but be careful, they're known for getting quite jealous!

People born in the Year of the Horse are very energetic and love to travel. But remember, they do not like waiting. They want to bolt right out of the gates!

GOAT

Also known as the Year of the Sheep, people born in this year can be a little shy but are great at understanding people. They're happy to be left alone with their thoughts, and maybe think a bit too much about what others think of them.

Monkeys are a lot of fun to be around. Active and entertaining, people born in this year are great at making people laugh! They like to listen to others but can sometimes lack self-control.

Hard-working and practical, those born in the Year of the Rooster have a bit of a reputation for being perfectionists. They're very reliable – you can always trust a rooster.

People born in the Year of the Dog are amazing friends and great at sharing. They sometimes get a little moody, but they're famous for being good, honest people.

What a great sign to be in! People born in the Year of the Pig are known for being luxurious! They love learning and helping others.

Q&A with M Chan

What is your zodiac animal?
I am a SSSssssnake!

Which of the zodiac animals' powers would you most like to use?
I would love to use invisibility! I could tickle people without them knowing who it was!

Would you like to be the Tiger Warrior?
I can't imagine myself protecting an entire kingdom like Jack does because it's a huge responsibility. I think he is very brave to take on that role. However, I would like to have some of his adventures and would definitely like to meet his friends in the Jade Kingdom such as Princess Li and the zodiac animals, as they seem like a lot of fun.

Have you ever been to the Jade Kingdom?
I haven't been to the Jade Kingdom yet. I hope to one day. I wonder if I need my passport?

Which baddy would you be most afraid to battle?
This question is easy to answer because it's Nian! I think it's a terrifying creature who eats children.

About M Chan

Maisie Chan is a children's author from Birmingham. When she was growing up, Maisie had no books that featured Chinese role models, so she became a children's author to change that. She even studied why there were not many Chinese role models in film at universities in Birmingham and America.

Maisie has been a storyteller in the past and entertained children in libraries, museums and schools with her favourite Chinese myths and legends. She currently lives in Glasgow and enjoys practicing yoga and walks around the parks and visiting the seaside.

THE TIGER WARRIOR NEEDS YOU!

Some children are lost in the maze. Can you help Li and Jack get to them without bumping into Nian?!

Read how it all began! Turn over to follow Jack as he becomes the Tiger Warrior in:

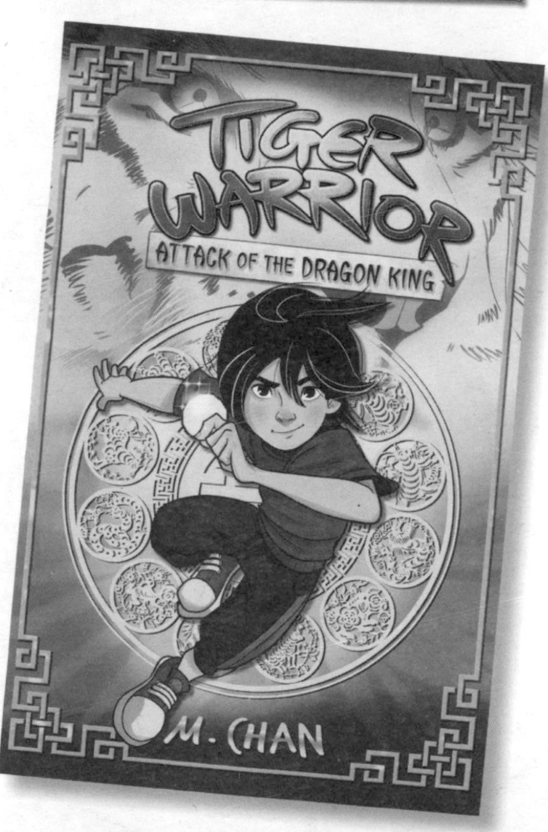

CHAPTER ONE

"Take that!" Jack yelled. He pressed the buttons on his controller and the game's green dragon exploded in a splatter of dust. But just as Jack thought he had won, an orange dragon flew out of a castle and began to attack his avatar.

"Oh, no you don't!" His avatar rolled away from the dragon's flames. "That was close!"

Jack's bedroom door opened and his grandpa, who he called Yeye, came in. He stood by the door, watching Jack playing his game. "Hi, Yeye," Jack said, not taking his eyes from the screen.

"That's not how to defeat a dragon," Yeye said.

"Oh, yeah?" Jack laughed, twisting around in his gaming seat to look at Yeye, whose eyes were shining mischievously.

"Do it like this!" Yeye sprang up, kicking hard, his slipper flying into the air and almost knocking Jack's lamp over. Jack's jaw dropped. "And then turn ... like this ... uppercut!" Yeye yelled as he punched into the air with surprising ferocity.

Jack grinned then swivelled back round to his screen. He pushed the buttons, trying to copy Yeye's moves. His avatar leapt, punching the dragon into oblivion.

"No way! It worked!" Jack turned to

see Yeye bent over, coughing as he made his way to Jack's chair.

"Yes! I told you!" Yeye said, taking breaths in between coughs.

Jack got up and went to his grandpa, whose face was going beetroot red.

"Shall I get some water?" Jack asked.

"No, don't worry about me. Just got something in my throat," Yeye choked out. "I'm fine."

Yeye didn't look fine. "I think you should rest," Jack said. "You're always saying you're not a spring chicken any more!"

"This old chicken could outrun you any day!" Yeye joked, stifling more coughs.

"But I think it's time, Jack ..."

"Time for what?" Jack asked, helping his grandpa to sit down.

"To pass on to you something which was Ju-Long's."

"Dad's?" Jack said in surprise.

Yeye nodded. "Which was your father's before he ..."

"Before he died." Jack sat down next to his grandad. "Yeye, is everything OK?" His grandpa was acting really strangely.

"Jack, are you brave enough to face a real dragon?" Yeye asked, looking deadly serious.

"There's no such thing! Yeye, I think you need to rest." Jack laughed.

"I'm serious ... I'm not going to be around for ever. It's time." Yeye grabbed hold of his arm. "Come to my room; I've got something special I need to give you. Before it's too late."

"OK, you're scaring me now." Why was his granddad acting so weird? Jack always felt a little knot in his belly when Yeye mentioned his dad. He'd died when Jack was one. Not long afterwards, Yeye had decided to move from China and come and live with Jack and his mum.

Jack shook his head as he followed Yeye to his room across the landing.

"Come! You will see!" Excitedly now, Yeye shuffled into his bedroom. Jack loved Yeye's room. It smelled tangy from his ointment, and the walls were covered in long scrolls with brush art pictures of dragons, as well as funny cartoons Yeye had cut out from newspapers. Yeye noticed Jack looking around. "Your father would have been happy that you were going to have it ..." Yeye pulled out a wooden box and opened it slowly. He held something in the palm of his hand, which he extended to Jack. "This is for you."

"Thanks, I guess ..." said Jack, taking the shiny pale green disc and turning it over.

Yeye reached out and cuffed Jack's ear.

"Oww!" Jack yelled. "What's that for?"

"Thanks, I guess? That was for your cheeky monkey talk. This is the Jade Coin, the most precious object in the universe!" Yeye looked different now, his face radiant as he gazed at the green thing in Jack's hand. "Look closely. What can you see?"

"Well ..." Jack said. He stared hard at the coin – he recognised the twelve creatures of the zodiac. Yeye had drilled into him the story of the animals and how they came to be in the Chinese Zodiac, and every bedtime he would tell Jack a different myth. "OK, so yeah, I see.

The Rat, Ox, Tiger, Rabbit, Dragon, Snake, Horse, Goat, Monkey, Rooster, Dog, Pig ... see, I was listening."

"Good!" Yeye chuckled. "I was going to wait until you were older, but you are right. I am no spring chicken – more like an old goose. I taught you about the ancient myths for a reason."

"To bore me to death?" Jack said, ducking before Yeye could cuff him again.

"Listen. Jack ... I have something to tell you." Yeye held his grandson's shoulders and stared into his eyes. "You are the Tiger Warrior! You must take up your place and battle the forces of evil in the Jade Kingdom."

Yeye paused dramatically. Jack rolled his eyes.

"If demons take over the Jade Kingdom, then our world will be next!" Yeye said urgently.

Jack laughed. "Yeah right, good one, Yeye!"

"I see that I'm going to have to convince you," Yeye said. With a quick flick of his fingers, he tossed the Jade Coin into the air. As it spun, it caught the light, filling Yeye's bedroom with colourful rainbows. It seemed almost ... magical.

"TIGER TRANSFORM!" Yeye shouted out loud. In a flash, he disappeared. And in his place was a huge, roaring tiger!

For fun activities and more about Jack and the Jade Kingdom, go to:

www.orchardseriesbooks.co.uk